Hattie's New House

Hattie's New House

LUCY DANIELS

Illustrated by DAVID MELLING

AN
APPLE
PAPERBACK

Scholastic Inc.

New York   Toronto   London   Auckland   Sydney
Mexico City   New Delhi   Hong Kong   Buenos Aires

To Sarah Bertram

Special thanks to Jan Burchett and Sara Vogler

ISBN 0-439-68196-0

Text copyright © 2003 by Working Partners Limited
Created by Working Partners Limited, London W6 0QT
Illustrations copyright © 2003 by David Melling

12   11   10 9   8   7   6   5   4   3   5   6   7   8   9/0

Printed in the U.S.A.   40
First Scholastic printing, November 2004

Look for these
LITTLE DOLPHIN titles:

Party Time, Poppy!
Milo's Big Mistake
Oscar's Best Friends

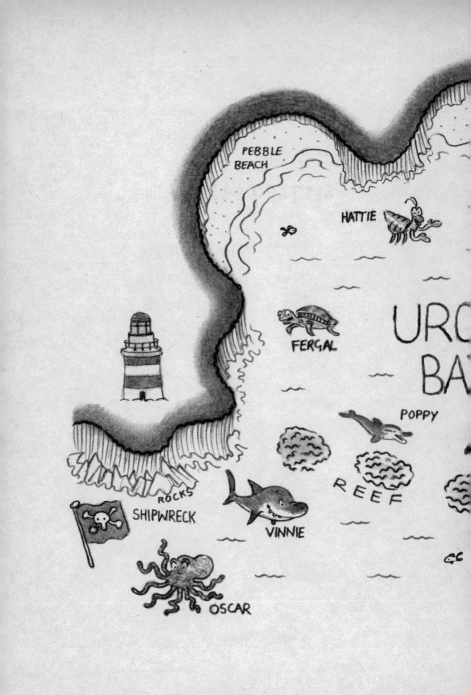

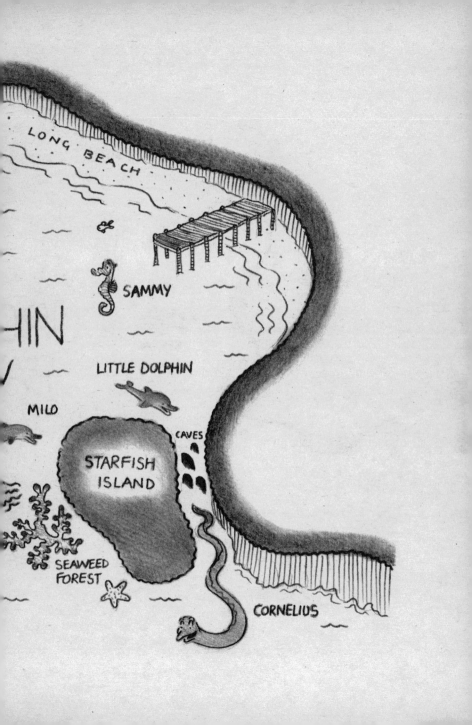

CHAPTER ONE

Little Dolphin poked his nose out of the water. It was a lovely morning in Urchin Bay. The sun was shining and the sea was blue. It was a perfect day for jumping.

Little Dolphin could see his best friend, Milo, in the middle of the bay. Milo was leaping out of the water. He curved in the air and then plunged back down through the waves. He made jumping look so easy!

Little Dolphin longed to be able to jump. He'd flipped his flippers and flapped his tail. He'd wiggled his whole body until he thought his head would fall off! But he still couldn't do a jump. Not even a tiny one.

"Come on, Little Dolphin!" called Milo. He swooshed past, backward, balancing on his tail. "Remember — nose up, tail flip, wiggle! See that clump of seaweed at the end of the reef? Jump over that!"

"I'll try," Little Dolphin said. It was only a small clump of seaweed after all. He could easily jump over that! He gave Milo a determined smile and set off, swimming along the coral reef. A family of clown fish darted away to hide in the pink and orange fingers of coral as he skimmed past.

Little Dolphin could see the seaweed straight ahead. It looked a lot bigger now. Could he really jump over that? He could feel his heart pounding. Little Dolphin put his nose up, flapped his tail, and wiggled. Oh, no! He was too close to the seaweed. He shut his eyes quickly, tried to swerve, and

plunged straight into the waving green leaves!

Milo pushed the sticky weed off his friend's flippers with his nose.

"Tough luck, Little Dolphin," he said.

Little Dolphin sighed. "All the other dolphins I know can jump. Why can't I?"

"You will," said Milo. He gave Little Dolphin a friendly nudge with his tail. "Try flapping your fins harder."

"I'm flapping as hard as I can," Little Dolphin said.

"Could you wiggle a bit more?" asked Milo.

"If I wiggle any more I'll burst!" Little Dolphin wailed. "I know what I'm supposed to do. It's just that I get all mixed up when I try."

Milo thought hard. "When I learned to jump, my brother Bertie gave me some very good advice," he said. "In fact, he told me never to forget it."

"Great! What was it?" Little Dolphin asked eagerly.

Milo thought again. Then he shook his head. "I forget!" he said.

Little Dolphin rolled his eyes. Milo was such a scatterbrain! "Well, my dad says I should just keep practicing," he said.

Milo nodded. "Your dad should know. He's been Urchin Bay's jumping champion for three years straight! His triple flips last Sports Day were the best!"

Milo rolled over and over in the water, scattering some passing angelfish. Suddenly, he snorted with laughter. "That was a great day! Do you remember Poppy in the Junior Spinner Dolphin Race?"

"Oh, yes," Little Dolphin said. "She spun so fast she got all dizzy

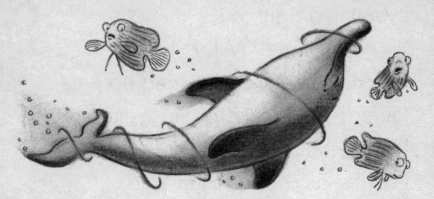

and ended up with her nose stuck in a clamshell! It was so funny."

"The clam didn't think so!" whistled Milo.

Little Dolphin grinned. Milo always cheered him up. As he looked out across Urchin Bay, he saw some more dolphins jumping and playing in the warm sun. "I'll try one more time," he decided. This time he was going to get everything right.

"Watch me, Milo!" Little Dolphin called, as he sped up toward the surface of the water. He lifted his head ready to soar into the air — and then Little

Dolphin forgot everything he'd been told. What should he do with his nose? And should he flap before he wiggled?

In a panic he flapped wildly, wiggled his nose, lifted his tail — and plunged straight to the bottom of Urchin Bay.

CHAPTER TWO

Ouch! Little Dolphin's nose hit
something hard and knobbly on
the sandy seabed. He darted
back, sending the sand swirling.

"Watch out!" said a grumpy
voice.

Where was the voice coming
from? Little Dolphin couldn't see
anything through the churning sand.

"I'm uncomfortable enough without dolphins landing on me!" said the angry voice.

Little Dolphin looked at the seabed. The sand was settling now, but all he could see was a shabby brown shell among the pebbles. "Who's there?" he asked timidly.

"It's me, silly!" The shell gave a shudder. Then a snapping claw appeared, followed by a pair of beady eyes and two twitching whiskers. Hattie the hermit crab was peering out at him.

"Hattie!" Little Dolphin whistled

in relief. "I didn't recognize you. You're living in a new shell! I'm sorry I landed on you. You see, I'm learning to jump. And I keep getting it wrong."

"Well, I've got a much worse problem," said Hattie impatiently. "This morning I decided that my lovely white shell had grown too tight. I think I've been eating too many sea slugs —"

Suddenly, there was a yell and a scraping noise behind them. They turned to see Milo skidding along on his belly. He crashed straight into them. Little Dolphin and Hattie were sent rolling over and over, along the seabed.

"Did you like my skid stop, Little Dolphin?" Milo clicked happily. Then he spotted Hattie shaking her claws at him. "Oh, hello, Hattie. What are you doing in that ugly old shell?"

"That's what I'm trying to tell Little Dolphin," grumbled Hattie. She struggled out of her shell and stretched her stiff legs with a groan. Then she went on with her story. "As I was saying, my white

shell had grown too tight, so I was looking for a new home. That shifty shark, Vinnie, told me he had just the shell for me. It only cost two limpets and a barnacle. So I paid up, and he took my lovely white shell away. But he tricked me! This brown shell is even smaller."

"And it's so scruffy, it looks like it's been in a fight with a swordfish!" remarked Milo.

Little Dolphin felt sorry for Hattie. He was glad dolphins didn't have to always find new homes. "Let's play a game of hide-and-seek," he chirped. "That will cheer you up."

"How can I play hide-and-seek when I've got to carry this heavy old shell around?" moaned Hattie. "I miss my shiny white one."

"Follow the leader, then?" squeaked Milo. "I'll go first." He began to twist in and out of the rocks on the seabed.

"I'm too slow in this horrible shell," complained Hattie. "Now if I had my white one . . ."

"Let's play tic-tac-toe," Little Dolphin said quickly. "You don't have to move much for that." He drew a grid in the sand with his nose.

"I don't want to play anything.
I'm too uncomfortable!" Hattie
snapped.

Little Dolphin felt a bit
impatient with Hattie. "OK,
Hattie," he said. "If you don't want
to play, Milo and I will do some
jumping practice instead."

"I knew there was something we were supposed to be doing!" whistled Milo.

Hattie struggled back into her tight brown shell. "Go ahead then," she muttered. "See if I care!" And she crawled awkwardly away.

CHAPTER THREE

Little Dolphin swam up to the
surface. "Nose up, tail flip,
wiggle!" he said to himself. "Nose
up, tail flip, wiggle . . . or is
it nose flip, tail wiggle?" He turned
to ask Milo.

Milo was playing in the waves,
batting a red beach ball between
his flippers. He had forgotten
about jumping. "Look what I've

found, Little Dolphin," he called. "It must have washed out to sea. Let's play a game!"

But Little Dolphin still wanted to jump. He decided to go home and ask his mom for another lesson. He said good-bye to Milo, who was balancing the ball on his nose in front of a group of admiring seal pups.

Little Dolphin set off toward the

rocks on the other side of the reef. He swam along, feeling the sun on his back and sending spray up through his blowhole.

Soon he was swimming over the hole in the reef where Cornelius the conger eel lived. Cornelius didn't like to be disturbed. Was that a big gray nose coming slowly out of the hole? With a flick of his tail, Little Dolphin swam quickly away.

He stopped and looked back to make sure Cornelius wasn't following him. Suddenly, he felt something pinch his tail! Little Dolphin was really scared.

"Ouch!" he cried. Then he felt
another pinch — and this time it
was harder!

Little Dolphin lifted his nose,
gave his tail a sharp flick — and
shot clean out of the water, up, up,
up into the bright sunlight!

CHAPTER FOUR

Little Dolphin couldn't believe it.
He was jumping! It was a great
feeling, soaring up toward the blue
sky.

His landing wasn't so good,
though. He hit the water with a
huge *smack!*

But Little Dolphin didn't care.
He had jumped! He had to tell
Milo!

Then he remembered his sore tail. Had Cornelius nipped it? Was he still lurking nearby? Little Dolphin looked back anxiously toward the reef.

There on the coral stood Hattie the hermit crab. She was waving her claws angrily at him.

"Did *you* pinch my tail, Hattie?" Little Dolphin asked in surprise.

"Yes, I did," snapped Hattie.

"But why?" Little Dolphin asked.

"Because I'm very uncomfortable in this *horrible* new shell," Hattie said. "And you don't care!"

"Yes I do, Hattie!" Little Dolphin squeaked. "And thank you for pinching my tail. It was very clever of you!"

Hattie's eyes stood out on their stalks. "What are you talking about?" she spluttered.

"When you pinched me," Little Dolphin said, "it surprised me so much that I jumped right out of the water. So now I know I really *can* jump. Look, I'll show you!"

Little Dolphin put his nose up, flapped his tail, and jumped. He got halfway out of the water and fell back in with a *splash*! "Now I'll show you a double twist just like my dad does." Flippers flapping wildly, Little Dolphin launched himself in the air, gave a twitch, and flopped back down in a storm of bubbles.

"And for my last trick," he called, "I'll —"

"Stop!" clattered Hattie. "You're making me dizzy!"

Little Dolphin looked at poor Hattie. She must be very unhappy in her cramped brown shell, he realized. No wonder she couldn't enjoy his jumping display. "I wish I could help you," he said. "After all, you helped me."

Milo was still playing around with the red beach ball across the bay. "Shall we go and play with Milo?" he asked. "That might cheer you up."

"I can't!" wailed Hattie. "It'll take me all day to get there in this shell."

Little Dolphin thought it was sad that Hattie couldn't go without her shell. But he knew that hermit crabs had to take their homes with them wherever they went.

Then he had a brilliant idea. "How about a ride?" he whistled. "Hang on to my fin and we'll be there before you can say lolloping lobsters!"

"I'll fall off!" clacked Hattie in alarm. "This shell isn't built for speed."

"I won't go fast," Little Dolphin promised.

Hattie looked doubtful. "OK," she said at last. "But remember — go slowly."

She climbed onto Little Dolphin's back and gripped his fin with both claws. "I'm ready," she called.

Little Dolphin set off, swimming slowly toward Milo.

"Are you OK, Hattie?" he asked.
He could feel her claws getting
tighter on his fin.

"Of course I am," said Hattie.
"Can't you go any faster?"

Little Dolphin grinned and
sped up.

"Yippee!" squealed his
passenger. "Faster, Little Dolphin!
Faster!"

They plowed through the water,
Hattie clinging tightly and yelling
with delight.

In no time at all, they reached
Milo. "I'll surprise him," Little
Dolphin said. "Milo doesn't know I
can jump."

"Watch me, Milo!" he called. And he launched himself out of the water.

"Aargh!" clattered Hattie as she lost her grip and went flying high in the air.

CHAPTER FIVE

Oops! Little Dolphin had forgotten all about Hattie. She came down with a splash and sank to the bottom of the bay. Little Dolphin sped after her.

Hattie's shell was wedged in the sandy seabed. Little Dolphin could see her whiskers waving helplessly out of the top.

"Hattie!" he squeaked. "Are you all right?"

For a moment there was no reply. Then Little Dolphin heard a hollow grunting sound from the shell. What could be wrong?

Slowly, Hattie pulled herself out of her shell. Now Little Dolphin knew what the strange noise was. Hattie was laughing.

"That was great!" she gasped. She scrambled eagerly onto Little Dolphin's back again.

Little Dolphin swam up to the surface with Hattie. Milo whistled with delight when they told him the story of Little Dolphin's first jump.

"One day I'll be like my dad," Little Dolphin said. "The best jumper in Urchin Bay!"

"Never," said Milo with a sassy grin. "Hattie will always jump higher than you!" And with a flick of his tail he was off. "Can't catch me!" he called as he charged through a family of surprised shrimp.

Little Dolphin sped after Milo, with Hattie on his back. Hattie held on tightly as they chased in and out of the seaweed. At last they sank down on some bouncy sponges.

"Thank you, Little Dolphin," said Hattie. "I've had a wonderful time. You really cheered me up." She clicked her claws and did a little dance in the sand. "In fact, I feel so much better I'm going to find that shifty shark Vinnie and tell him to give me back my limpets and barnacle. See you later." And off she went.

"I'm glad Hattie cheered up," grinned Milo. "Race you to the wreck, Little Dolphin!"

"I've got a better idea," Little Dolphin

declared. "Let's play Hunt the Shell."

"Hunt the Shell?" said Milo, puzzled.

"We're going to find a new house for Hattie," Little Dolphin explained.

The two friends swam up and down, nosing in the sand.

"What about this?" called Milo. He nudged a rusty old can along the seabed. "It's really modern, and if she gets tired of walking, she can close the lid and roll instead."

"Hattie won't like that!" Little Dolphin answered. "Keep looking."

Milo grinned and poked around in some seaweed. Then he swam into a gap in the coral. "Help me with this, Little Dolphin!" he called as he wriggled out backward.

Little Dolphin swam over. Milo was tugging at something long and thin.

"I've found a new kind of seaweed," Milo said.

Little Dolphin saw what Milo

had in his mouth. "That's not seaweed!" he squeaked. "Quick, we have to hide!"

They darted behind the leaves of a large kelp bush.

Milo looked puzzled. "What's the matter?" he whispered.

"You were pulling Cornelius's tail!" Little Dolphin told him.

"I was?" squeaked Milo in surprise.

"Yes, and now he's coming this way!" said Little Dolphin.

They sank down onto the sand and tried their best to look like seaweed-covered rocks as the old conger eel slid past. He had a

grumpy frown on his face, and Little Dolphin was sure he was searching for whoever had pulled his tail.

Milo started to wriggle.

"Keep still," Little Dolphin clicked. "He'll see us."

"But I've got an itchy nose!" Milo clicked back.

At that moment, Cornelius turned and swam toward them. Little Dolphin and Milo froze. They felt a swish of water as the conger eel swam right over them, muttering to himself.

After a while, they couldn't hear him anymore.

Little Dolphin risked a peek.

"He's gone," he sighed. "We'd have been in trouble if he'd found us."

But Milo wasn't listening. He was rubbing his itchy nose all over the seabed.

As he did, Little Dolphin could see something appearing from under the sand.

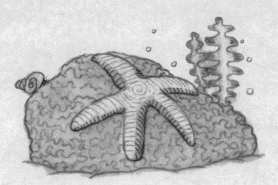

CHAPTER SIX

Little Dolphin quickly flapped away the rest of the sand. And there in front of him was a shell. A beautiful, pearly pink shell. "You've found a house for Hattie!" he whistled.

"I have?" asked Milo in surprise.

"Yes, you have," Little Dolphin said. "We have to give it to her!"

Balancing the shell carefully on his nose, Little Dolphin swam off to find Hattie, with Milo close behind.

The hermit crab hadn't gone very far. "Wait, Hattie!" Little Dolphin called.

Hattie kept inching her way across the seabed. "No time for playing now, Little Dolphin," she said.

"But we've got a present for you!" said Milo.

Hattie stopped and turned slowly around.

Little Dolphin put the shell down in front of her.

Hattie couldn't believe her eyes. "It's beautiful!" she gasped. She scrambled out of her old brown one and scuttled into the lovely pink one. "And it's a perfect fit!"

"Now don't eat too many sea slugs!" grinned Milo.

Hattie pranced proudly up and down to show it off. "Thank you, Little Dolphin!" she said. "Thank you, Milo. I could win the Hermit Crab Marathon in this."

The two dolphins rubbed noses in delight.

"What are you going to do with the old one?" Little Dolphin asked.

Hattie looked thoughtful. "We'll give it back to Vinnie," she said at last. "I've thought of a great joke to play on that shifty shark."

Five minutes later, the three friends were watching secretly from behind a clump of sea cucumbers as Vinnie the shark danced in and out of his cave. He was singing the Sharky Sharks' latest hit as he decorated his dinner with sea parsley.

"See my eyes flashing in the dark!" he sang happily. "Here I am, I'm a sharky shark!"

"He's in a good mood!" Little Dolphin clicked. "Maybe he'll give you back your limpets and barnacle if you ask him nicely, Hattie."

"I will," said Hattie with a twinkle in her eye, "after we've played our joke. Ready, Milo?"

Milo was batting Hattie's old shell between his flippers in time to Vinnie's song. "Ready for what?" he asked.

"Our joke on Vinnie!" Little Dolphin hissed.

"Oh, yes!" grinned Milo. "I forgot!"

As soon as Vinnie went back inside his cave, Milo darted forward, hid the shell in Vinnie's dinner, and then dashed back to his hiding place. He was just in time.

Vinnie glided out of his cave, his beady eyes glancing all around. Then he opened his mouth as wide as he could. The whole pile of food disappeared in one enormous bite.

Suddenly, there was a loud *crunch*! Vinnie was so surprised he spat his dinner all over the seabed.

Now it was time for Little Dolphin's part of the plan.

He popped out from behind the sea cucumbers and swam around Vinnie, pretending to search for something. "Have you seen Hattie, Vinnie?" he asked. "She was taking a nap — around here somewhere."

Vinnie's jaw dropped open. He looked at the remains of his dinner and spotted the bits of Hattie's old shell. In a panic he pushed them around with his nose. "Hattie!" he cried. "Speak to me, Hattie!"

He turned to Little Dolphin. "Jumping jellyfish!" he gulped. "I've

eaten her. And she was one of my
best customers!"

Little Dolphin
couldn't help
grinning.

"It's not
funny!" wailed
Vinnie.

"Yes, it is!" said
Hattie. She scuttled out
of her hiding place, followed by
Milo. Her whiskers twitched with
amusement.

"Hattie!" gasped Vinnie.
"You're alive!" Then he noticed that
the two dolphins were rolling

about with glee. "Hopping halibut!" he exclaimed. "You tricked me!"

"Just like you tricked *me* into buying that horrible shell this morning," snapped Hattie. "You knew it was too small for me."

"It's not my fault if you've grown since breakfast," blustered Vinnie. "What's all the fuss? You seem to have found a new one."

"No thanks to you!" said Hattie. "I want my limpets and barnacle back, please."

"I don't do refunds," said Vinnie. "But what about an

exchange? I happen to have a nice razor shell, just in. Only one owner —"

"Don't be mean, Vinnie," Little Dolphin clicked. "Give Hattie what you owe her."

"She can't use her old shell," added Milo. "You've eaten it!"

"All right, all right!" said Vinnie. "Don't get your flippers in a twist." He swam into his cave and came back with two limpets and a barnacle. He dropped them in front of Hattie and gave her a toothy smile. "While you're here," he said, "you might be interested

in a bargain." He produced a
small glass bottle. "Claw polish,"
he explained. "Just your color. And
it's yours for only —"

"No, thank you," interrupted
Hattie firmly. "I've had enough
bargains for today."

"Fair enough," said Vinnie
cheerfully. "Now if you ever want

to sell that new shell, I'll give you
a good price."

"I'm not parting with this one in
a hurry!" said Hattie. "I want to go
and show it to everyone. Can I
have a ride please, Little Dolphin?"

"Hop aboard, Hattie!" Little
Dolphin grinned.

"That was a great joke,
Hattie!" said Milo as the three
friends swam along the reef.

"I'll never forget Vinnie's face
when he thought he'd eaten
me," Hattie clacked. "Thanks for
helping, boys — and my new
house is great."

"And thank you for helping me

learn to jump, Hattie," Little
Dolphin responded.

"You may be able to jump,"
said Milo with a grin, "but I bet
you can't jump as high as me!"

"Bet I can!" Little Dolphin
called. "Hold on tight, Hattie!
We're off!"

And the three friends raced off
to leap in and out of the waves.